Yaffa Ganz

PURIM

WITH BINA, BENNY AND CHAGGAI HAYONAH

This book belongs to:

_____

The ArtScroll Children's Holiday Series

⑤

Yaffa Ganz

PURIM

WITH BINA, BENNY AND CHAGGAI HAYONAH

Illustrated by Liat Benyaminy Ariel

SHALOM, welcome to the Royal Roost! I am Chaggai, King of the Doves, and Purim is on its way! Actually, I'm really only Chaggai Hayonah — the holiday dove — but on the 14th of Adar, everything changes. Ordinary boys and girls suddenly turn into kings and queens, old men, young brides, milkmen, soldiers, Indians, and even traffic lights and ice-cream cones!

I wonder what my friends Bina and Benny dressed up as this year? Hmm. . . that queen and the prime minister standing next to her look familiar, don't you think?

"Do you have the *groggers,* Benny? May I have the blue one. It matches my veil."

Benny handed the blue noisemaker to his sister.

"Don't you think," continued Bina, "that someone as good and wise as Mordechai should have been the king instead of Achashveirosh?"

"That would have mixed up the entire Purim story!" cried Benny as he straightened his beard. "Besides, there were no Jewish kings in Persia!"

"There was a Jewish queen," said Bina.

"But no one knew she was Jewish," insisted Benny.

"Hashem knew!"

"Indeed He did," nodded Chaggai the dove. "But at first, only Mordechai the Jew, who had been one of the Sages in the *Sanhedrin* in Jerusalem, understood what was happening. It was like this. . .

 ong ago, over two thousand and three hundred years to be exact, a new king arose in the land of Persia. Achashveirosh was his name. He had conquered many lands until he ruled one hundred and twenty-seven provinces, all the way from Hodu to Kush. His capital city was called Shushan.

"Where's that?" interrupted Benny.

"Hodu is India. That's in Asia. And Kush is Ethiopia. That's in Africa," whispered Bina.

Achashveirosh built himself a new throne in Shushan. To celebrate, he made a tremendous feast for all the important people in the kingdom. It lasted one hundred and eighty days. Then he made a second feast just for the city of Shushan. Everyone in the city was invited, even the Jews. For seven days they ate and drank to their heart's content. Even the dishes were special. Achashveirosh served the food and wine on holy vessels from the *Beis Hamikdash*.

"How did vessels from the *Beis Hamikdash* get to Shushan?" asked Bina.

"Nevuchadnezzar had destroyed the *Beis Hamikdash* seventy years before," said Chaggai. "Many of the gold and silver vessels were brought to Babylon. Now all of Nevuchadnezzar's treasures belonged to Achashveirosh."

"Did the Jews eat at Achashveirosh's feast? Did they drink his wine? Did they use the holy dishes?" asked Benny.

"Yes, they did," answered Chaggai sadly. "The wise Mordechai had warned them not to go to the feast, but they were afraid to disobey the king."

The seventh and last day of the feast in Shushan was on a Shabbos. By now, Achashveirosh was quite drunk. He didn't know what he was saying or doing. He bragged that Vashti the queen was the most beautiful of all women, and he commanded her to dance before his guests to prove it.

Vashti was from a royal family, a granddaughter of Nevuchadnezzar. And she would not follow the king's orders. "Am I the king's servant?" she asked haughtily. She refused to appear, and the angry king had her killed that very day.

"Poor Vashti," said Benny.

"Don't feel sorry for her," said Chaggai. "Vashti was a cruel queen. She hated the Jews as much as her grandfather Nevuchadnezzar had hated them. She even forced Jewish girls to work on Shabbos, just out of spite!"

"Is that why she was killed on a Shabbos?" asked Bina.

"Indeed it was," agreed the dove.

But now the king needed a queen and so the search began. Soldiers went from province to province, from city to city, from house to house. The fairest young women in Persia were brought to the palace where they lived for an entire year, making themselves beautiful and waiting for the king to choose a new queen.

In the city of Shushan, a Jewish orphan by the name of Hadassah, who was also known as Esther, lived with her cousin Mordechai. When the king's men came to take Hadassah to the palace, Mordechai said, "Do not be afraid. Go with them to the palace, but do not tell them the name of your nation or family. Trust in G-d and He will watch over you."

When she went to the palace, the only thing she would say was, "My name is Esther." Achashveirosh saw Esther, and immediately chose her as the new queen of Persia, the most beautiful and special of all the women in the kingdom.

Esther appointed seven maidservants, one for each day of the week, so that she would remember which day was Shabbos. Her meals were cooked in her own private kitchens, so she would eat only kosher food. And all the while, she kept her secret. No one knew that Esther was a Jew.

chashveirosh had ministers and advisors galore in the royal court, and Esther, who wanted Mordechai to be near the palace, suggested to the king that he appoint a Jewish advisor as well. She knew just the person — a wise and loyal Jew by the name of Mordechai!

One day, while at his new job, Mordechai happened to hear two of the king's servants, Bigsan and Seresh,

planning to poison the king. Mordechai quickly warned Esther. Bigsan and Seresh were caught and put to death. It was duly recorded in the Royal Book of Chronicles that Mordechai the Jew had saved the life of the king.

Soon after, Achashveirosh appointed Haman, the richest man in the country, as his prime minister. The king was so impressed by his wealth that he ordered everyone in the palace to honor Haman by bowing down to him. People were afraid of Haman and whenever they saw him, they bowed down, long and low. Everyone except Mordechai.

Haman wore a large medallion with a picture of an idol.

"If I bow to him," said Mordechai, "it will look as though I am bowing down to the idol. A Jew does not bow to idols."

Haman was furious. He swore he would destroy not only Mordechai, but all of the Jews, and off he went to the king.

"Your Majesty," he said, "there is one nation scattered throughout your kingdom which is different from all other nations. They don't eat our food, nor drink our wine, nor will they marry our daughters. Even worse, they don't keep the king's laws! And they are lazy, always pretending to celebrate their Sabbaths and holidays. If only the king will grant me permission, I will destroy them forever."

The thoughtless Achashveirosh couldn't have cared less. "Do as you like," he said. "Here — take my royal ring to seal your orders."

Achashveirosh may have been thoughtless, but Haman was not. He thought and planned and thought some more, and he finally cast lots — *purim* in Hebrew — to choose the perfect day for his plan. Then he sent out letters, sealed with the king's royal ring, to each of the hundred and twenty-seven provinces.

"On the 13th day of Adar," wrote Haman, "you are to destroy, kill and slaughter all Jews, young and old, women and children, everyone, in one day. You can keep their money and property."

"That's scary!" said Benny.

"It sure is," said Bina.

The Jews thought it was scary too. "It's because of the *treif* food we ate at Achashveirosh's feast!" they said. "It's because we drank non-kosher wine! It's because we used the holy vessels of the *Beis Hamikdash!* Who can save us now???"

Mordechai knew there was only one way they could be saved — through G-d's help. He fasted and prayed and ripped his robe as a sign of mourning. Then he put on sackcloth and spread ashes on his head and sat down outside the palace gate.

When Esther heard that Mordechai was sitting in the middle of town in dirty, torn clothing, she sent him new robes and asked him to come to her palace. But Mordechai refused. Instead, he sent Esther a copy of Haman's decree and asked her to go to the king and try to save the Jews.

One couldn't just walk in to see the king, however. One had to be invited, and Esther had not been invited for thirty days.

"Perhaps the king will not want to see me," she said. "He might even kill me if I enter without permission."

"Do not think, my child," said Mordechai, "that your life will be saved if the Jews die. If you do not come forward to help now, someone else will fill your place. Perhaps this is the reason you were chosen as queen!"

"Then I will go," said Esther. "But first, let all the Jews in Shushan fast and pray for me for three days."

So all the Jews of Shushan fasted and prayed. They begged Hashem to forgive them for their sins, to have pity on them, and to save them from Haman's decree.

Mordechai gathered twenty-two thousand Jewish children. He learned Torah with them and prayed with them. G-d heard their voices and said, "For the sake of the children, I will save my people!"

The three days of fasting were over. It was time for Esther to go to the king. When Achashveirosh saw Esther at the entrance to his throne room, he was so surprised and pleased that he held out his scepter as a sign that she was welcome!

"Why have you come, Esther?" he asked. "What would you like? Whatever you desire, up to half my kingdom, it shall be yours for the asking!"

But all Esther asked was that the king and Haman come to a dinner she was preparing. Achashveirosh wondered why Haman was invited, but perhaps Esther just meant to honor the king by inviting his prime minister. Haman, however, was absolutely delighted. What an honor! A private invitation from the queen herself!

At the banquet, Achashveirosh asked Esther again, "Is there something, anything at all, you wish? You have but to tell me and it is yours." Once again, Esther only replied, "I would like the king and Haman to come to a second banquet tomorrow."

By now, the king was really getting curious. But Haman left the palace in a wonderful mood. At least it was wonderful until he bumped right into Mordechai! As usual, Mordechai refused to bow, and Haman's smile melted right away. "How I hate that Jew!" he muttered.

Haman went home and told his family about Esther's party. But he could not enjoy his good luck so long as Mordechai the Jew was sitting at the palace gate.

"I wish I could kill Mordechai now!" he said to his wife Zeresh, "without waiting until the 13th of Adar!"

"Then do it!" she said. "Build a gallows and hang him immediately. Surely the king will not object. If he granted you permission to kill all the Jews in the kingdom, what will he care if one Jew dies sooner?"

Haman was so pleased at his wife's suggestion that he began building a gallows, fifty cubits high, in his own back-yard.

hat night, no one slept. The Jews were busy praying. Haman's family was busy building a gallows for Mordechai. The Persians were busy thinking of how they would soon be killing Jews and taking their money. Only Achashveirosh was fast asleep. Hashem saw him and said, "Why should this evil king sleep so peacefully while my children are suffering?" and he promptly woke the king.

Achashveirosh tossed and turned but he could not fall back asleep. He began to think. He wondered why Esther had invited Haman not once, but twice, to her banquets. Could he trust Haman? Whom could he trust? Perhaps he should be paying more attention to his kingdom. Achashveirosh told his servant Shamshi to bring out the Royal Book of Chronicles and read to him.

Shamshi was one of Haman's sons, and when the Book of Chronicles opened to the story of how Mordechai had saved

the king, he quickly turned to another page. He didn't want
to read anything good about his father's most hated enemy!
But no matter how many pages he turned, the book always
opened to the same spot. Finally, the king lost his patience.

"Why are you fiddling around?" he shouted. "Just read!"

"Um . . . the words are blurry," mumbled Shamshi.

Suddenly, the words seemed to read themselves. In a
clear, soothing voice, they read all about Bigsan and Seresh
who wanted to poison the king. When the story was over,
Achashveirosh asked, "And what reward did Mordechai
receive for saving my life? What?" he cried. "Nothing?
Nothing at all for saving the king's life? How can that be?"

Just then, who should appear, in the middle of the night,
but Haman himself! He was in such a hurry to ask the king's
permission to hang Mordechai the Jew that he didn't even
wait for the morning.

"Haman!" cried the King. "Just the man I need!"

"Haman, think carefully and tell me. What shall be done for a man whom the king wishes to honor?"

"Hmm," thought Haman, "whom would the king want to honor but me!

"I know just what you should do, your majesty," he said. "Let him wear the king's royal robes and put the royal crown upon his head. Let him ride the king's own horse, and have a herald walk before him and announce: Thus shall be done to the man whom the king desires to honor!"

"I bet Haman could just see himself on that royal horse," said Benny.

"I bet he could!" giggled Bina.

"Splendid," said the king. "Now see to it that every single thing you have said is done for Mordechai the Jew! And do it quickly!" When the king gave an order like that, even Haman got moving!

Haman found Mordechai sitting in his sackcloth and ashes near the palace gate. He took Mordechai home. He cut his hair and washed and perfumed and dressed him in the king's royal clothes, the very ones Haman had hoped to wear himself. When the king's horse arrived, Haman even bent down so that Mordechai could step on his back and mount!

"Ah me," sighed Haman. "And I wanted Mordechai to bow down to me!" He straightened up, made sure that Mordechai was sitting comfortably, and began to lead the horse through the streets of Shushan.

"Thus shall be done to the man whom the king desires to honor!" cried Haman in his loudest voice as royal guards and heralds marched in a magnificent procession through the city. Absolutely everyone came out to see them. Haman's daughter came too. She went up to the roof of her house with a pail of garbage, ready to throw it on Mordechai's head. (She thought Haman would be riding the horse!) When she threw it on her father by mistake, she was so upset, that she fell right off the roof of her house!

When it was all over, Haman returned home, a broken man. But he didn't have much time to mull over his misfortunes. He had to hurry to the queen's second banquet.

The party began. Once again, the king asked the queen, "What is it you desire, Esther? Why have you invited us here? Ask what you will. Even if it is half my kingdom, it shall be yours." This time, Esther was ready to speak.

"Your majesty," she cried, "spare my life and the lives of my innocent people! We have all been sentenced to die!"

"What? The queen? Sentenced to die? Who has done such an evil thing? What traitor is at work here?"

"A wicked and sinful man! This evil Haman!" cried Esther, pointing to the surprised minister. The king was so astounded that he jumped up and out to the garden.

Haman knew that all was lost. He threw himself on Esther's couch to beg for mercy just as the king marched back into the room.

"What is this? Are you attacking the queen now? Right

here? In my palace? Seize him!!!" he shouted.

The guards grabbed Haman, and one of them, Charvona by name, said, "Does the king know that Haman built a gallows fifty cubits high to hang the loyal Mordechai?"

"Well then," cried the enraged king, "hang him on his own gallows!"

Mordechai became the prime minister in place of Haman, and for once, Achashveirosh had a good idea of his own.

"Take my signet ring," he told Esther and Mordechai. "No one may change a decree which was stamped with the royal seal, so even I cannot cancel Haman's decree against the Jews. But if you can think of another way to save the Jews, you may use my ring for a new decree."

Mordechai called for the scribes and sent out a royal decree to all the people in the kingdom: On the thirteenth of Adar, the Jews would organize and arm and defend themselves against their enemies! Mordechai left the king dressed in royal clothing, with a large gold crown on his head. And the Jews of Shushan were cheerful and glad.

But many other people were afraid. They were happy to kill the Jews if the king and Haman told them to do so, but if the king had changed his mind, and if the Jews were going to fight back, then perhaps it was better for to stay quietly at home!

On the 13th of Adar, the Jews rose up across the kingdom and killed many thousands of their enemies, including Haman's ten evil sons who were hung from a tree. On the fourteen of Adar, they gave thanks to Hashem and celebrated their victories.

In Shushan, however, there was not enough time to finish the battle. So Esther asked the king for one more day to fight. And on the 15th of Adar, the Jews in the walled city of Shushan celebrated. That's why the 15th of Adar is called Shushan Purim.

Mordechai wrote the story of Purim in a *megillah* — a scroll — and he sent a copy to all the Jews in the kingdom. He commanded them to keep Purim forever as a day of gladness and joy, feasting and sending gifts to our friends and to the poor. And that's just what we've done for over two thousand, three hundred years.

"I know where we still celebrate Shushan Purim," said Benny. "In Yerushalayim!"

Chaggai smiled. "Good for you, Benny!"

"What else should we know about Purim?" asked Bina.

"You should know that Taanis Esther — the Fast of Esther — is the day before Purim," said Chaggai. "And on Purim day, there are four main mitzvos."

1. *KRIAS HAMEGILLAH* — Reading the Megillah
2. *MISHLOACH MANOS* — Sending a gift of two portions of food to at least one friend or neighbor
3. *MATANOS L'EVYONIM* — Gifts of money for the poor
4. *SEUDAS PURIM* — Eating the Purim meal

"The first mitzvah is tonight," said Benny. "Reading the Megillah!"

"That's only half of the first mitzvah," said Bina. "We read the Megillah tomorrow morning too."

"I know. And both times, my friends and I intend to make plenty of noise whenever Haman's name is mentioned. We'll stamp our feet and turn our groggers."

"Just remember," Chaggai warned, "the noise is only for Haman. You have to be quiet for the rest of the Megillah. Otherwise you won't hear all the words."

"What kind of noise will you make, Chaggai?" asked Bina. "You don't have a grogger like we do."

"Why, I'll flap my wings and toot, of course."

"I think Abba and Imma are calling us, Benny. Come on. It's time to go to shul!"

"id you hear me tooting in shul?" asked Chaggai.

"Not quite. It was pretty noisy. But your costume is super!"

"Thank you," cooed the dove shyly. "Even a dove likes to look a little different on Purim. I do make a rather fearful Haman, don't you think? I wanted to be Mordechai's horse this year, but it's so hard to turn a dove into a horse. I'm missing two feet."

"A horse? You?" Benny started to laugh.

"It's no funnier than a boy being a bear, is it?" asked Chaggai. (Benny had been a bear last Purim.)

"Of course it's not!" said Bina quickly. "On Purim, anyone can be anything he or she wants. Even a dove. And when we carry the *shalach manos* tray with you sitting on top, we're going to look perfectly elegant. No one else has a Haman-dove bringing *shalach manos*."

"Is the tray ready?" asked Benny. "I hope Imma made some of those delicious chocolate balls."

"Of course she did. And she made batches and batches of hamantashen too, shaped just like Haman's three-cornered hat."

"Personally, I like the sesame cookies best," cooed Chaggai.

"Did Abba give *matanos l'evyonim* yet? asked Bina.

"Sure," answered Benny chewing a chocolate ball. "He gave it to the *rav* right after the Megillah reading this morning. The rav already gave it to two poor families he knows. Do you have the *shalach manos* list, Bina?"

"Here it is. Let's see, we're going to the Goldbergs and the Levines and Mrs. Meyers at the Old Age Home. And to Aunt Judy and Uncle Chaim. And of course to our friends. And this year, Benny, you carry the tray and I ring the doorbells. I can't wait to see if anyone recognizes us!"

"Well, if everything is ready," chirped Chaggai, let's go!"

 sn't it lovely? Such a wonderful time of bringing gifts and giving tzedakah and celebrating and being happy. The Purim seudah in Bina and Benny's house is enough to make your head spin — so many songs and stories and jokes about Purim. So many cousins and friends; such delicious food and cake and wine.

Bina and Benny are happy and thankful. They know that even in time of danger, if the Jews guard the Torah and keep its laws, Hashem will guard and bless and take of them.

On Purim, they especially remember that all Jews are part of one family, one people. We love and help and take care of each other. We share good times and bad, troubles and joys. And if we remember these things, G-d will give us light, and gladness, and honor and joy, just like the Jews in the story of Purim. So . . .

PURIM SAMEACH
A HAPPY AND JOYOUS PURIM

from me, Bina,
and me, Benny, and me,
Haman — oops! I mean. . .
Chaggai the holiday dove!

GLOSSARY

Abba — father

Adar — the twelfth and last month of the year

Am Yisrael — the Nation of Israel

Beis Hamikdash — The Holy Temple in Jerusalem

berachah — a blessing

Eretz Yisrael — The Land of Israel

grogger — (Yiddish) a noisemaker used on Purim

hamantashen — (Yiddish) three-cornered, filled cookies

Imma — Mother

Hashem — G-d

megillah — a hand written scroll on parchment

Megillah — the Scroll of Esther

mishloach manos — a gift of two portions of food sent to a friend or neighbor on Purim

mitzvah, mitzvos — a commandment, commandments

rav — rabbi

Sanhedrin — the High Court in Jerusalem

Shabbos — the Sabbath

shalach manos — mishloach manos

shekel — the standard coin in ancient and modern Israel

shul — (Yiddish) synagogue

sofer — scribe who writes Torah and Megillah scrolls

Taanis Esther — the Fast of Esther

treif — not kosher

tzedakah — charity

Yehoshua — Joshua

Yerushalayim — Jerusalem